Goosebumps®

PRESENTS

Have you seen the show on Fox Kids TV? It's creepy. It's spooky. It's funny. . . . It's GOOSEBUMPS!

Don't you love GOOSEBUMPS on TV? And if you do, then you'll love this book, *The Headless Ghost*. It's exactly what you see on TV — complete with pages and pages of color photos right from the show! It's spook-tacular!

So check under your bed, pull your covers up tight, and start to read *The Headless Ghost*. GOOSEBUMPS PRESENTS is so good . . . it's scary!

Look for more books
in the GOOSEBUMPS PRESENTS series:

Goosebumps®

PRESENTS

THE HEADLESS GHOST

Adapted by Carol Ellis
From the teleplay by Billy Brown and Dan Angel
Based on the novel by R.L. Stine

SCHOLASTIC INC.
New York Toronto London Auckland Sydney

A PARACHUTE PRESS BOOK

Adapted by Carol Ellis, from the teleplay by Billy Brown and Dan Angel. Based on the novel by R.L. Stine.

ISBN 0-590-93954-8

Photos courtesy of Protocol Entertainment © 1996 by Protocol Entertainment.
Text copyright © 1996 by Parachute Press, Inc.
All rights reserved. Published by Scholastic Inc.
GOOSEBUMPS is a registered trademark of Parachute Press, Inc.

12 11 10 9 8 7 6 5 4 3 2 1   6 7 8 9/9 0 1/0

Printed in the U.S.A.   40

First Scholastic printing, December 1996

Midnight at Hill House
January 1880

"Are you here?" twelve-year-old Andrew whispered. He held his breath and stood very still.

Was the ghost hiding in here? Watching him?

Andrew gazed around his dark bedroom. "If you're here, show yourself," he demanded.

The candle on Andrew's nightstand flickered. The beam from the nearby lighthouse flashed across his bedroom walls.

Nothing else moved.

And no one answered.

"Where are you?" Andrew asked impatiently. He tiptoed around the room. He peered into the shadowy corners.

A hand suddenly reached out and grabbed his shoulder.

"Ahhhh!" Andrew yelped and spun around.

His mother stood in front of him. She wore a long white nightgown. She frowned.

"Why are you still dressed?" she asked.

Andrew glanced down at his knickers and high-collared shirt. He shrugged.

"And why aren't you in bed, Andrew?" she continued.

Andrew put an innocent expression on his face. "I was just going, Momma," he lied.

His mother glared at him. "Hmmph," she grumbled. "A likely story. You're looking for that ghost again, aren't you?"

"No, Momma. Honest."

"I don't know why you believe those stories," his mother scolded. "There is no ghost in this house. Now go to bed."

"I will," Andrew promised. "Good night, Momma."

His mother frowned at him again. Then, finally, she left the room.

Andrew waited for a moment. He listened at the door. No, his mother wasn't going to come back.

Then he smiled.

"Come on, you stupid old ghost," he whispered. "I'm not afraid of you!"

Andrew stood in the center of his room.

Listening.

There it was! A scratching noise! It came from under the bed.

Andrew's heart pounded with excitement. I knew it! he thought. I knew that dumb ghost was in here!

The noise stopped. Andrew waited. The scratching started again.

Andrew crept quietly across the room. He bent down slowly, very slowly. He peered underneath the bed.

A pair of glowing eyes stared straight back at him.

Andrew gasped. He clutched the bed frame to keep from falling over.

Then a little voice said, "*Meow.*"

"Oh, it's only you, kitty." Andrew sighed in disappointment.

As he stood, he heard something. Another sound.

Only this time it was right behind him.

Andrew whirled around.

But all he saw was the shadowy darkness.

"Who's there?" he called.

Silence.

Suddenly, a cold wind whistled through the open window. The candle sitting on the nightstand blew out. With a shiver, Andrew turned.

And froze in horror.

Floating before him was a ghost. A huge, horrible ghost. He wore a peacoat and a sea captain's hat.

Andrew's heart pounded in terror as he gazed at the ghost's hideous face. "No! Please!" he choked out.

The ghost spoke in a low, raspy voice.

"Now that you have seen me," the ghost growled. "You can never leave."

The ghost took a step toward him.

Andrew couldn't move.

He couldn't even scream as the long, icy fingers reached for his head.

2

"Reaching. Reaching. The ghost's fingers stretched closer to Andrew's head." Otto's voice dropped down to a creepy whisper.

I love this part of the story. I'm Duane Comack, and I've been taking the tour of Haunted Hill House ever since I was a little kid. I'm twelve now, so I must have heard this same story a gazillion times.

We were all crowded into the old-fashioned bedroom. Otto, the tour guide, was doing his usual job of scaring the tourists.

"Then what happened?" an older woman asked. She looked nervous. *All* the tourists looked nervous. Some of them even seemed scared of Otto!

Otto is definitely weird-looking. Some-times he scares even *me*. He is huge, with a gleaming bald head and bushy whiskers on his face. And his tiny black eyes seem to stare right through me.

"What did the ghost do?" the woman asked in a shaky voice.

"Yeah! What happened to Andrew?" another tourist called out.

Otto didn't answer. He was making them wait. He always does that. It made the story even scarier. He gazed at the tourists' faces. Then he shut his eyes, as if what he was about to say was truly terrible. Finally, he took a deep breath.

"The ghost yanked Andrew's head off!" he boomed.

The crowd gasped. Then Otto's eyes popped open. His voice shook. "And he hid the head somewhere in this very house," he went on.

Otto was putting on a good show today! He sure knows how to tell a ghost story.

"Every night since then, Andrew's ghost

7

wanders these halls, searching for his missing head," Otto continued in his creepy voice.

A frightened little girl whimpered. She hid behind her mother's skirt.

"It's just a story," her mom assured her. "It's all part of the tour. It's just pretend."

Otto waved his arm toward the door. "Now if you will follow me, we will view the rest of the house. And who knows?" he added with a sly smile. "Perhaps tonight the headless boy will pay us a visit."

Otto strode to the door. We all swarmed after him. As I passed by the bed, I thought I noticed something move. I glanced down.

And froze.

A hand reached out from under the bed!

A green, gross, slimy hand with long blue fingernails.

My mouth dropped open as I watched the hand stretch farther and farther. Then the hideous fingers wrapped around the little girl's ankle!

"Ahhhhh!" The little girl shrieked in terror. Her mother yanked her out of the grasp of the disgusting hand. The little girl wailed with fear, clutching her mother's legs.

The other tourists stopped and turned. When they saw the slimy hand, some gasped and some screamed.

I stood there, frozen in horror.

Otto spun around in the doorway. "Stand back!" he yelled. He pushed the frightened tourists aside and marched to the bed.

I scrambled out of his way. Otto knelt down and peered under the bed.

"All right, come out of there," he demanded. "You come out of there right now!"

Slowly, someone slid out from under the bed. But it wasn't a monster or a ghost.

It was Stephanie Albert.

My best friend.

Stephanie leaped to her feet. She was laughing really hard. She snatched the fake hand off her arm. She bounced over to the little girl and waved the gross hand in her face.

"No! Mama!" the little girl shrieked.

"You stop that right now," the girl's mother yelled at Stephanie.

Stephanie just laughed harder.

I shook my head. This time Stephanie went too far. It's one thing to frighten big kids and grown-ups. But Stephanie shouldn't scare such a little girl.

Still, I had to admit it was a cool trick. It even scared me!

And I'm one of the Twin Terrors!

That's what we call ourselves. Stephanie and I are always coming up with jokes to play at Hill House. Once we hid in a closet and made spooky moaning sounds. Another time, we smeared our faces with glow-in-the-dark paint and crept around in the shadows.

But I was getting kind of sick of the Twin Terrors. It didn't seem like much fun anymore. In fact, it seemed kind of dumb. And now Otto was going to be furious.

I glanced at him. His face was bright red. Boy, was he mad.

He grabbed Stephanie by the arm. Then he yanked me by the collar.

"Hey! What did I —" I stammered.

He dragged me and Stephanie out of the room and to the front door of the house.

"Out!" he shouted. He released his grip and pulled open the door. "Out with you now!" He pushed us through the front door onto the snow-covered steps. "One day you kids are going to realize that the spirits who haunt this house don't enjoy pranks."

Stephanie opened her mouth to talk back, but one nasty look from Otto shut her up.

"Don't come back until you're ready to show Hill House and its ghostly guests some respect!"

Otto slammed the door in our faces. He slammed it so hard, the haunted house sign shook. Even the door knocker — an ugly twisted goblin face — seemed to glare at us.

I scurried down the block. I wanted to get out of there — fast. I had never seen Otto so serious. It sounded as if he actually believed the house was haunted! As if he thought Stephanie and I were annoying the ghosts who lived there.

It bugged me that Otto was mad at *me*. I didn't even do anything. It was all Stephanie's fault.

Stephanie burst out laughing. She skipped along behind me. "That was excellent!" she cried. "Did you see the look on that little girl's face?"

I stopped and frowned at her in the moonlight. "You went too far this time, Steph," I told her. "She was really scared."

"That's the point, Duane!" Stephanie argued. "The Twin Terrors of Wheeler Falls strike again!"

I sighed. "Maybe we're getting a little old for this Twin Terrors stuff."

Stephanie looked shocked. "Are you nuts?" she cried. "We're just getting good!" Then she grinned. "I know! Let's come back tomorrow night. We'll sneak away from the tour. Then we'll search for the head of Andrew the Headless Ghost!"

I didn't like this idea. Otto was really mad. He would probably still be mad tomorrow.

And what if he was right? What if there *were* spirits who didn't like our pranks?

I shook my head. You're being ridiculous, I told myself. There's no such thing as ghosts!

Still . . .

"I don't know, Stephanie."

She rolled her eyes. "What? All of a sudden you're afraid of Otto the Odd?" She stared at me as if I were a total dweeb.

I glanced back at the house. I had the creepiest feeling we were being watched.

But no one stood in the windows. The yard was empty. It must just be my imagination.

Even so . . .

"I don't know, Steph," I repeated. "Besides, you heard what Otto said. The ghosts don't like our tricks."

She snorted. "You believe that?"

"I didn't say that. I . . ."

"You what?" Stephanie demanded.

"I don't know," I said again.

"Are you scared?" Stephanie asked. She gazed at me with narrowed eyes.

"No!" I practically shouted. But it was a lie. For some reason, I *was* a little nervous. Maybe it was the prickly feeling crawling up my neck. The feeling I get if someone is spying on me.

But I could never admit I was scared to Stephanie. She wasn't afraid of anything. And I knew she would tease me about being a wimp.

"Come on, Duane!" Stephanie insisted. "It will be great!"

I glanced back at the house. A beam of light from the lighthouse flashed across the windows. The tall scraggly bushes cast creepy shadows on the snow.

My heart stopped.

What was that? Hidden in the bushes by the front door.

I was right! Someone was watching us.

There, peering from the shrubs, was a pale white face. The face of a boy about my age. With strange glittery blue eyes.

I only saw him for a second. The lighthouse

beam moved past the house. When it flashed again, there was no one there.

Should I say something to Stephanie? I wondered.

Maybe I just imagined the boy. Maybe it was just the light playing tricks.

Maybe.

Stephanie was still talking about her great idea to sneak away from the tour group. "Tomorrow night Hill House will definitely be haunted," she declared. "By us!"

I nodded. But why did I have the terrible feeling I was going to regret this?

3

I was more afraid of Stephanie's teasing than I was of ghosts.

So there I was, back at Hill House the next night. Stephanie and I hid behind the crowd in the main hall. A new group of tourists listened and shivered with fear as Otto retold the old Hill House ghost stories.

For some reason, I shivered along with them.

The wind rattled the tree branches outside. Heavy gray clouds blew across the moon. Tonight Hill House actually feels haunted, I thought.

Stephanie glanced at me. I smiled weakly. I didn't want her to know how nervous I felt.

"The history of this house is one of madness and despair," Otto announced in his big dramatic voice. Stephanie rolled her eyes.

"This house was built by a sea captain over one hundred and fifty years ago," Otto continued. "He built it for his ladylove. But when he came back from a sea voyage he discovered his beloved had left him for another man."

This was one of Otto's boring stories. And one I knew by heart. I mouthed the words silently along with the big tour guide. Stephanie struggled to keep from laughing.

"The poor captain died of a broken heart." Otto made his voice sound sad. I put a sad expression on my face. "But his angry spirit lived on, taking revenge upon anyone who dared live in his house."

I must have been making a funny face because Stephanie snorted. Otto spotted her in the crowd and glared at her. "The sea captain's spirit took revenge on anyone who mocked the ghosts within," he bellowed. Then he flashed us a mean smile. "I'm glad to see our regulars have decided to behave themselves tonight. For their sake."

Of course, Stephanie didn't pay attention to Otto's latest warning. Instead, she stuck out her tongue when Otto turned his back.

Otto waved his arm and the crowd moved toward the staircase. Large oil paintings hung along the walls all the way up.

"Each of these portraits represents some poor soul who tried to live in this house," Otto explained. He began climbing the stairs. The tourists followed. "And then each died a horrible, grisly death."

Otto stopped in front of one of the paintings. Some of the tourists gasped in horror.

I smiled. It was a painting of Andrew, the Headless Ghost.

Well, that's not exactly right. He had a head. It just wasn't attached to his neck.

Andrew carried his head in his arms.

"If you'll follow me," Otto instructed, "you will hear the bloody story of a young lad named Andrew. A lad who lost his head."

The crowd followed Otto up to the second

floor. He led them to the bedroom where he always tells the story of Andrew and the ghostly sea captain.

Stephanie and I hung at the back of the group. As the group crowded into the bedroom, we stayed right outside the door. We waited for the perfect moment to sneak off.

Otto began the story. Stephanie rocked back and forth on her feet. I could tell she was getting impatient.

Finally, Otto reached the scariest part of the story. "The ghost's long, icy fingers reached toward Andrew's head," he whispered.

The tourists stood frozen, waiting to hear what happened.

"Now's our chance!" Stephanie murmured to me. "Come on!"

Quickly, she slipped under a velvet rope and started down the hallway.

I stared after her. *Move*, I told myself. But my feet stayed where they were.

I didn't want to sneak away.

And it wasn't because I was afraid, either.

It was because I didn't want to get into trouble when we got caught.

"What happened?" a tourist yelled out.

Stephanie stopped and turned. She must have noticed I wasn't following her. "Come on!" she urged.

There was no way to back out now. I tiptoed after her.

"This will be *too* cool," Stephanie whispered excitedly.

From behind me, I could still hear Otto's voice. "The ghost pulled Andrew's head off!" he boomed.

"Do you think Andrew will thank us when we find his head?" Stephanie joked.

"If Otto doesn't rip off *our* heads first!" I answered.

Stephanie giggled.

As we wandered down the long, dark hallway, I had that weird feeling again, the feeling that we were being watched.

Just like last night, I thought, when I spotted that pale boy hiding in the bushes.

Could that same boy be spying on us now? I peered into the shadowy corners.

You're being a dope, Duane, I scolded myself. There's nothing there. No one. It's only your imagination.

I hurried to catch up with Stephanie. She stood outside the captain's study.

"Ready?" she said in a low voice.

I nodded.

Stephanie pushed on the door.

Creeeaaak. The door opened slowly. Stephanie grinned at me. Then she stepped into the dark room.

I took a deep breath and followed her inside.

The moon shone through the window. It was the only light in the room, except when the lighthouse beam passed through.

Suddenly Stephanie gasped. "Oh, no!" she whispered. "Oh, no!"

My heart started to pound. "What?" I croaked.

She stared at something in the corner.

"The . . . the head!" Stephanie's voice shook with fear.

My heart thumped even harder. And then my palms began to sweat. But I had to see. I had to see Andrew's head!

"Where?" I was so scared my voice squeaked.

Stephanie burst out laughing. "Nowhere!" she cried. "D-uh, Duane. Are you going to fall for every dumb trick tonight?"

Stephanie could be a real jerk sometimes. Even if she was my best friend.

"Don't do that!" I snapped. "It's not funny!"

But she didn't answer. She stared past me, over my shoulder. Her face twisted in horror. "Duane!" she said. "I'm not kidding this time. Look!"

"Where? What?" I whirled around. "Is it the head?"

I scanned the dark room. I could make out the shadowy shapes of tall bookcases, a couch, and a large wooden desk.

No head.

I glanced at Stephanie.

She gazed back at me, a huge grin on her face.

I slapped a hand to my forehead. "Oh, man," I moaned. "I can't believe I fell for that *twice*!"

Stephanie laughed so hard she doubled over. I was about to give her a good hard shove when I heard something.

I froze. "What was that?" I hissed.

"Don't even try it," Stephanie said between giggles.

I waved a hand at her. "*Shhhhh*. Listen!" I insisted.

Stephanie quieted down. We stood in the dark, listening.

There it was again.

Now I recognized the sound.

Footsteps.

Footsteps coming closer.

Stephanie and I stared at each other, our mouths open.

"Something's coming!" Stephanie cried.

"Now what do we do?" I exclaimed.

Stephanie ran to the closet and yanked

open the door. "In here!" she whispered. "Quick!"

I raced across the room and darted into the closet. Then Stephanie stepped in and pulled the door shut behind her.

Just in time.

I could hear the door to the study creak open. Then *thump, thump, thump,* the footsteps crossed the room.

Thump thump thump.

The footsteps stopped right in front of the closet door.

I glanced at Stephanie. She looked terrified.

A rattling sound caught my attention.

The doorknob.

The doorknob was turning slowly.

Then the closet door flew wide open!

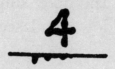

4

My stomach lurched as the closet door burst open.

A horrible face stared back at me.

A twisted, huge face, red with fury! Tiny beady black eyes glittering with anger!

With a bald head that gleamed in the moonlight.

Otto.

Without a word, he yanked me and Stephanie out of the closet.

I didn't think a guy that big could move so fast! Otto dragged us out of the study, down the hall, down the stairs, and out onto the sidewalk in front of Hill House.

"You are no longer welcome at Hill

House!" Otto shouted from the doorway. "And if you ever do come back, I won't be responsible for what the spirits might do! You have no respect."

Otto slammed the door shut with a bang. Stephanie bent down and scooped up a big handful of snow.

"Respect this, you old grouch!" she hollered. She hurled the snowball at the house.

"Don't!" I grabbed at her arm but it was too late. The snow and ice exploded against the goblin face on the door knocker. "What did you do that for?" I demanded.

"What's your problem?" she asked.

"What's yours?" I yelled. She was getting me mad.

Stephanie sighed. "You know, Duane, you're turning into a real drag."

"*I'm* a drag?" My voice rose in anger. "You never know when to stop, do you, Stephanie? One day you're going to get us in major trouble."

"Yeah, yeah, yeah," she muttered.

I ran my hand through my hair. I didn't want to fight with Stephanie. She was my best friend.

"Oh, forget it," I grumbled. "Let's just get out of here."

We turned down the sidewalk. But someone stood in our path, blocking our way.

A boy about my age. A pale boy with weird blue eyes.

The boy I saw last night, watching us from the bushes.

"Do you want to see real ghosts?" the boy asked. He had a low, soft voice.

"Who are you?" I asked. He gave me the creeps.

The boy smiled. But it wasn't a very friendly smile. "My name is Seth," he answered.

"I'm Stephanie." Stephanie grinned at the kid. "And this is Duane."

She didn't seemed bothered by Seth at all. She seemed to like him right away.

I didn't trust him. Why was he hiding in the bushes? Why did he spy on us?

Seth took a step closer. "I heard you talking about the Headless Ghost last night," he said. "If you really want to see him, you have to wait until after the tourists go home." He smiled again. "That's when the good stuff happens."

"How do *you* know?" Stephanie demanded.

Seth glanced around. He lowered his voice. "I sneaked in," he told us. "Late one night. I waited until —"

Before Seth could finish, the door to Hill House started to open.

"Quick!" Seth whispered. "Over here!"

Stephanie and I darted behind him into the bushes. We ducked down in the shrubs. Silently, we watched the tourists leave Hill House.

When the last of the group disappeared down the path, Seth grinned at Stephanie and me. "I know a way in through the basement." His smile widened. "Should we sneak in tonight?"

I'm Duane Comack, and I think Hill House is the coolest place in Wheeler Falls. That's because it's a <u>haunted</u> house.

My friend Stephanie and I hang out there all the time. We love taking the Hill House tour with the sightseers who visit our town.

Stephanie likes to pull pranks during the tours. Once, she put a fake monster claw on her hand and nearly scared a little girl to death.

I play jokes sometimes, too. But usually I go to Hill House to listen to the ghost stories.

Otto is the tour guide. His favorite story to tell is the tale of the Headless Ghost. . .

A long time ago, a boy named Andrew lived in Hill House. Andrew knew the house was haunted, and every night he searched for the ghost.

Andrew called the ghost names to make it mad. Then one night, he went too far. Andrew gasped in horror!

The ghost appeared and reached for Andrew with its long, icy fingers. He pulled Andrew's head right off!

One night, Stephanie made fun of the painting of Andrew that hangs in Hill House.

Otto got mad. He told us to have respect for the ghosts. Then he threw us out of Hill House!

Outside, we met a strange boy named Seth. He dared us to sneak back into the haunted house after dark.

We crept inside. Seth led us into the attic. "Do you want to meet a real ghost?" he asked.

Stephanie and I said yes. "Well, get ready," Seth told us. "Because you'll never believe the <u>real</u> story of the headless ghost. . ."

Stephanie's eyes lit up. "Yes!" she said instantly. "Let's do it!"

My stomach began to feel a little funny.

Seth looked at me. Stephanie was also waiting for me to answer.

"To-to-tonight?" I stammered. "Hmmm. Maybe tomorrow would be better."

Seth sneered at me. I guess he could tell I was stalling. "If Duane doesn't want to," he told Stephanie, "he doesn't have to. Not everyone can handle a real ghost hunt."

"Well, I can handle it!" Stephanie announced. She and Seth grinned at each other.

As if they were best friends.

"Hey, I never said I couldn't handle it!" I said. They were making me feel like a real wimp. "I'm a Terror Twin!"

"Then it's all settled," Seth declared. "We'll sneak back in when the coast is clear."

"And show those ghosts a thing or two!" Stephanie bragged.

"Careful, Stephanie," I warned her. "Remember what Otto said."

But she didn't pay any attention to me. She and Seth were too busy whispering. Then Seth pointed at the house.

All the lights went out.

A chill crept up my spine.

Hill House was closed for the evening.

But our night was just about to begin.

5

I don't like this, I thought. I don't like this at all.

Seth, Stephanie, and I stood in the front hall of Hill House. I couldn't see them — it was pitch black.

But I could *hear* Stephanie. She was giggling like she always does when she's excited.

"Hey, ghosts," she called. "Come out, come out wherever you are."

"Aren't you afraid?" I heard Seth ask.

Stephanie snorted. "Hah! Those ghosts should be afraid of *me*!"

A tiny flame appeared. A match. Seth held

it to a candle. The candle's flame gave Seth's pale face an eerie glow.

"*Shhhh,*" Seth whispered. "We don't want to wake the spirits." He grinned at me. "Yet."

He was such a creep.

But I couldn't let him know how nervous I felt. So I grinned back.

"Come on!" Using his candle to light the way, Seth started up the main staircase. Stephanie eagerly followed him. I took a deep breath and forced my feet to move forward.

I've been up those stairs dozens of times. But never in the middle of the night, when the only light was a tiny little candle flame.

And I've seen every one of the paintings we passed. A bunch of times! They never bothered me.

But tonight, all the eyes seemed to be watching me.

We reached the top of the stairs, and Seth led us down the dark hall. We tiptoed past Andrew's bedroom and the sea captain's study. Then we took a turn down another hallway. Doors lined the hall and each one was shut.

"I've never seen this part of the house," Stephanie murmured.

"It's not on the tour," I told her.

Seth's candle flickered. I hoped it wouldn't blow out. I didn't want to be left in Hill House without any light at all!

"None of these rooms are on the tour," Seth whispered. "You two are in for a special treat."

Great. I wasn't sure I wanted a special treat — not in a haunted house!

But Stephanie giggled. She didn't seem scared at all.

Seth came to a door and pushed it open. We followed him inside. He lit candles all around the room. They cast weird shadows on the walls. But at least I could see!

We were in an old-fashioned bedroom. There was a bed and a chest of drawers. An old croquet set sat beside me.

I reached out and touched a mallet. A

bunch of croquet balls fell and rolled across the floor.

The sound echoed through the house.

"Oops," I said.

"Way to go, Duane." Stephanie rolled her eyes.

"Sorry," I muttered.

A sudden cranking noise made me jump. I glanced across the room. Seth was turning some kind of handle on the wall.

"What's that?" Stephanie asked.

Seth opened a small door next to the handle. I hadn't noticed it before. It was about half the size of a closet. It reminded me of a mini-elevator.

"It's called a dumbwaiter," Seth explained. "It was used to bring food up from the kitchen. Lots of old houses have them."

"Neat." Stephanie darted across the room to join Seth by the dumbwaiter.

"Stay back!" Seth said sharply.

"Huh?" Stephanie froze.

"What's wrong?" I asked.

Seth gazed at us, a serious expression on his pale face. "I just don't want Stephanie to suffer the same fate as the poor boy who once lived in this room."

I knew Seth was only trying to scare us. The trouble was, it was working. At least on me.

"Was it Andrew?" I asked. "The boy who lost his head?"

"No," Seth answered. "Another boy. A boy about your age. He lived in the 1920s."

"So, what happened?" Stephanie asked.

Seth sighed. "Poor boy. He loved ice cream. Especially strawberry. And because he was very rich, he could have as much as he wanted."

"Good deal," Stephanie said.

Seth shook his head. "One day he demanded ice cream. Just like he always did. As usual, the maid put the silver bowl of strawberry ice cream into the dumbwaiter. Just as she always did."

Seth's voice was getting lower and lower. I

could tell he was coming to a scary part of the story. I wished there was some way to cover my ears without Stephanie or Seth noticing.

"The boy waited impatiently for his ice cream. But for some reason, the dumbwaiter didn't make it all the way up to the door. The boy peered into the shaft. He leaned over, trying to see why the dumbwaiter was stuck. He leaned out farther and farther."

Seth paused.

Even though I knew it was just a story, I felt afraid.

Finally, Seth continued. "Then, the boy stretched out too far!"

I shut my eyes. Bad idea. All I could picture was a boy lying splattered at the bottom of the dumbwaiter shaft. My eyes popped open.

"When the maid looked into the shaft, she screamed in horror," Seth finished. "It was hard to tell the difference between the boy's face and the strawberry ice cream he'd landed on."

"Gross," I muttered.

"Some say the boy fell. Some say he was pushed." Seth paused for a moment, then he smiled. "By a ghost," he added.

"That's just a story," Stephanie complained. "You promised you would show us real ghosts!"

I glared at Stephanie. She didn't have to remind him!

"Are you ready?" Seth asked.

"You bet!" Stephanie cried.

I wasn't so sure.

Seth must have noticed I wasn't saying anything. He sneered at me. "You don't have to come if you don't want to," he said.

He was just waiting for me to wimp out. No way!

"Of course I'll come!" I declared. I sounded a lot braver than I felt.

"Then we have to go upstairs," Seth told us. "To the captain's secret room."

"Cool!" Stephanie exclaimed. "What are we waiting for?"

"Yeah," I grumbled. I tried to sound excited. I wanted them to think I wasn't scared at all. "What are we waiting for?" I added. "Let's go!"

Seth led us up another flight of stairs. Halfway down the hall, he stopped in front of a tall dresser. He pushed it to one side.

Hidden behind the dresser was a staircase.

A very dark and narrow staircase.

Stephanie let out a low whistle. I gulped.

"After you, Duane," Seth said. Then he shoved me.

I stumbled up the first few steps. Then I got my balance and slowly climbed the stairway. Behind me, Seth's candle flickered. Our shadows on the walls danced like huge monsters.

At the top of the stairs I came to a small door. I had no choice. I had to open it. Stephanie and Seth were right behind me.

I took a deep breath and turned the handle. I flung open the door. I peered inside. It seemed to be a small attic. A skylight let in the glow of the moon.

"What gives, Duane?" Stephanie asked impatiently.

"Move!" Seth ordered.

"Okay! Okay!" I snapped. I stepped into the room. Stephanie and Seth pushed past me. The attic room grew brighter. I turned and noticed that Seth had lit an old-fashioned lantern.

I gazed around the room. The floors and walls were old, weathered wood. Fishing nets and a harpoon hung on the walls. An old peacoat and a captain's hat perched on a coat-rack. A sea chest sat against one wall. Against another wall stood a stack of blank artist's canvases.

I turned to Seth. "What are those canvases for?" I asked.

He grinned. "They belong to the captain's ghost," he explained. "They say he always paints his victims."

Stephanie laughed. "Yeah, right. A ghostly sea captain who paints in his spare time. Really believable, Seth."

Seth glared at her. That was the first time I saw him look mad. It sent chills down my spine.

Then he shrugged. "I'm just telling you what the story is. It's how the captain turns his victims into ghosts. He paints their portraits. And once the painting is done, the person has turned into a ghost." He waved toward the door. "All those paintings downstairs," he continued, "were painted by the captain."

I was sick of scary stories. Okay, so maybe I *am* a wimp. But I wanted out. "Listen," I said, not really caring what they thought. "It's getting late. We should go."

Seth crossed to the door. I couldn't believe he actually listened to me! I followed him. I wanted to get out of this stupid place.

But Seth didn't walk out the door. Instead, he shut it.

Then he pulled a key from his pocket.

And locked the door.

Suddenly, I didn't feel very well. I glanced at Stephanie. She gave me a puzzled frown.

"I'm sorry," Seth said softly. "I can't let you leave."

Stephanie crossed her arms and glared at

him. "What are you talking about?" she demanded.

"W-why did you lock the door, Seth?" I asked.

"I'm afraid I have a confession to make," Seth said. He turned to face us. "I lied to you. Sorry."

He didn't look sorry. He was smiling.

"What do you mean?" Stephanie asked.

"I mean my name isn't Seth. It's Andrew. Just as it was over one hundred years ago. When I lived in this house."

My mouth dropped open. But I guess Stephanie thought Seth was just pulling a prank. She snorted. "You can't be Andrew," she insisted. "How dumb do you think we are? You have a head. Andrew lost his head. Everybody knows that!"

For a second I felt better. Of course! Stephanie was right. Who did Seth think he was kidding? Stephanie and I knew all the stories.

Seth laughed. A really creepy laugh. An evil laugh.

"This isn't my real head." He choked out the words, he was laughing so hard. "I borrowed it. But I have to return it. So now I need a new one."

Suddenly he stopped laughing. He turned to me, deadly serious.

"And Duane," he said, taking a step toward me, "I'm going to take *your* head."

6

Seth walked toward me. One step. Another step.

"I need your head, Duane," Seth repeated.

"I need it, too!" My voice shook with fear.

"It won't hurt," Seth said. Then he paused as if he were thinking about it. "Well, maybe a little," he admitted. "But just for a second. One quick twist and it will come right off. Snap! Just like a chicken leg."

This can't be happening, I told myself. "You're joking, right?" I tried to laugh, but it sounded more like a croak.

Seth shook his head. "No joke, Duane. I'm going to pull off your head. I need it."

"Wait!" I pleaded. "Maybe we can help you. We can find your old head."

"It's no use," Seth told me. "For years I've searched every room. Every hallway. Every closet."

"But . . . why *my* head?" I asked.

Seth glanced at Stephanie. "Well, I'd take *her* head, but it would look funny."

Stephanie nodded quickly. "It would look terrible," she agreed.

Thanks a lot, Stephanie, I thought. She was no help!

I had to think of something! "But my head's not so great!" I cried. "It gets allergies! It's terrible at math. Its hair is always a mess!"

Seth just smiled. "Sorry, Duane. It's not going to work. I'm taking your head. That's all there is to it."

I took another step backward. And hit the wall behind me. There was nowhere left to go. And still Seth came toward me.

He stretched out his arms toward my head. "Now hold still."

My heart pounded and I felt sweat trickling down the back of my neck. Terrified, I glanced around the room.

Right beside me hung one of the old fishing nets. I yanked it hard. It ripped loose from the wall.

With a yell, I flung it over Seth's head and shoulders.

"Quick, Stephanie!" I shouted. "The dumbwaiter. It can take us down!"

We bolted across the room. I yanked open the dumbwaiter door.

Stephanie gasped.

I froze in horror.

Inside the dumbwaiter sat a head.

Andrew's missing head.

7

Stephanie shrieked.

I was too terrified to make a sound.

The eyes in the head glowed with a strange light. Then, as we gazed at it in horror, its lips moved. "What were you expecting?" the head snapped. "A dish of ice cream?"

I stumbled backward a few steps. Then I whirled around. Seth had already gotten free of the fishing net. He stood there, laughing.

"There's your head," I shouted. "Now you don't need mine!"

But he didn't answer. His pale face tilted up. He stared toward the ceiling.

I glanced up, too.

Something pale floated above us. It looked

like smoke or mist. Slowly, it drifted toward the floor.

As it got lower, the mist grew thicker. It formed into the body of a boy.

The boy wore a high collar and old-fashioned knickers. But the body had no head!

As I stared, the body moved. It lurched toward me.

"Yikes!" I scrambled out of its way.

"Hey! Over here!" a voice called from the dumbwaiter.

The head! It was shouting to the body.

"This is too weird," Stephanie muttered.

The body stumbled to the dumbwaiter. It stretched out its hands and picked up the head.

And dropped it.

"Ow! Oooh!" the head screeched as it rolled across the floor. "Clumsy fool!"

The body threw up its hands as if it were saying it was sorry. Then it tripped over to the head and picked it up.

"Easy! Easy!" the head griped. "It's a head, not a bowling ball!"

I glanced at Stephanie. She stared at the head, amazed.

"What are you looking at?" the head asked Stephanie. It sounded annoyed.

"Who, me?" she replied.

"Don't play innocent with me!" the head warned. "Or you'll find that my bite is worse than my bark!" It clicked its teeth up and down.

Stephanie quickly looked away.

The body carefully tucked the head under its arm and strode toward the door.

The head sniffed the body's armpit. "Pee-yew! When was the last time you took a shower? A hundred years ago?"

The body just kept walking.

If I had a head like that, I don't think I'd even *try* to find it.

I watched, stunned, as Andrew's head and body disappeared. Right through the wall.

"Whoa!" I gasped. I wanted out of there. I grabbed Stephanie's arm. I didn't care anymore if she teased me for being a wimp.

But Stephanie yanked her arm out of my

grasp. She turned to Seth. "You're not Andrew the Headless Ghost," she declared accusingly. "So who are you?"

"I'll tell you who he is!" a new voice boomed.

Stephanie and I spun around.

Otto loomed over us. He looked furious.

Uh-oh, I thought. We're really in for it now. Even Seth looked a little nervous.

"He's a no-good kid who works for me," Otto explained. "I warned you about these pranks," he added, turning to Seth.

I glanced toward the door — could we make a run for it? Then I noticed something strange. The door was still closed! I stared at Otto. "How did you get in here?" I asked him. "The door is locked."

"There are many ways to get into a room at Hill House," Otto replied mysteriously. "But sometimes there is no way out."

I didn't like the sound of that. And I didn't like the nasty gleam in Otto's beady black eyes as he approached me and Stephanie. My throat went dry when Otto's arms reached toward us.

But he didn't grab us! He just unlocked a different door behind us and swung it open.

Hooray! Escape! I was so relieved I could have kissed Otto.

Well, almost.

Otto led me to the door. "Good night, Duane," he said. He actually sounded friendly! Then he stepped in front of Stephanie. "Now, Stephanie, I would like to have a word with you. Alone."

I stopped. Why did Otto want to talk to Stephanie? Was he going to yell at her? Part of me wanted to race out of there and never look back. But Stephanie was my friend. I didn't want to leave her alone to get in trouble.

But Stephanie didn't seem worried. "Go ahead, Duane. I'll catch up with you."

"Are you sure?" I murmured.

She snorted. "Quit looking so scared," she scolded me. "What is Otto going to do — lecture me?"

"Please, Duane," Otto said in a soft voice. "Time to be going."

I slowly left the room, and Otto closed the door behind me. I peered into the shadowy darkness. It was pitch-black — I could hardly see my feet. I stumbled down a few steps and stopped.

I should have asked Seth for a candle, I thought. How was I going to see my way out?

I didn't have long to worry about it.

A terrified scream rang through the house. Stephanie!

8

"Stephanie!" I cried. But I was so frightened it came out as a whisper.

The blood-curdling scream came again.

I raced back up the stairs to the attic door.

The door was closed, but not locked. I pushed it open a crack and peered inside.

And gasped.

The Headless Ghost was back!

It sat beside Seth on the sofa, holding the head in its lap. Seth and the head both smiled as they gazed at Stephanie. She stood in the center of the room. She had a terrified look on her face.

Why isn't she moving? I wondered.

Otto stood near her. But now he wore the

clothes of a sea captain. He held a paint-brush. Beside him was an easel, with a canvas resting on it. He dabbed at the canvas with the paintbrush.

"I could really go for some strawberry ice cream," Seth said.

"Don't you ever learn?" the head demanded. "Didn't ice cream get you into enough trouble?"

My heart pounded in fear. I couldn't believe it! Seth was the boy who fell down the dumbwaiter shaft!

Seth was a ghost. Just like Andrew.

No wonder Stephanie looked terrified! She must have realized she was stuck in a room full of ghosts!

Otto ignored Seth and the Headless Ghost. He put a few more brushstrokes onto the canvas. What is he doing? I wondered. What is he painting?

I leaned forward to peer at the canvas.

My stomach flip-flopped.

He was painting a portrait of Stephanie!

That was why she couldn't move! Otto was

the ghost of the sea captain. The one who painted portraits of his victims. He was turning Stephanie into a ghost!

I thought I was going to throw up. But I couldn't. I had to do something to save my best friend.

The captain's eyes darted back and forth between Stephanie and the portrait. "When you become a permanent member of our little household, you'll learn," he told her in an icy voice. "Don't you think she'll learn?"

"Oh, yes!" Seth said. He snickered.

"She'll learn," the head agreed.

"Please," Stephanie whispered. Her voice sounded weak and distant. "I didn't mean to cause trouble. I'll never do it again."

"Of course you won't," the captain told her. "I'm making sure of that!" He dabbed some more paint onto the canvas.

Seth's terrifying words came back to me. *Once the painting is done, the person has turned into a ghost.*

I glanced back at the canvas.

The painting was almost finished!

I gazed at Stephanie. Oh, no! She was beginning to disappear! It was happening already.

Stephanie was turning into a ghost!

"Just one more dab around the mouth," the captain murmured as he examined his painting.

I couldn't let him finish. I flung open the door and charged into the attic.

"Duane! Help me!" Stephanie shrieked.

But I could hardly hear her.

I could hardly see her!

She was almost gone!

How can I stop this from happening? Do something! screamed my brain.

I know! Maybe if I knock the brush out of his hand!

I ran toward the captain's ghost. I had to stop him before he put the last bit of paint onto the canvas. But I stumbled over a bucket on the floor. Some kind of clear liquid sloshed onto my shoes.

I recognize that smell, I thought. I sniffed. Yes!

Paint remover.

The captain brought the paintbrush closer to the painting.

Closer.

Closer.

I grabbed the bucket of paint remover and hurled it at the canvas.

Splash!

Paint remover washed all over the painting. The paint smeared and dripped down the canvas.

"Noooooooooo!" the captain roared.

Stephanie came back to life! Her color returned in a rush. I couldn't see through her anymore. She was okay!

The captain moaned. Seth and the head wailed, too. The head floated up toward us. The sea captain and Seth reached their arms toward us, shrieking and shouting.

"Run!" I screeched at the top of my lungs. I yanked Stephanie's arm.

We bolted through the door and raced down the dark stairs. We rushed along the hallways, skidded around corners, and sprinted for the main staircase.

The ghosts chased after us, roaring and howling in fury.

We clattered down the steps at full speed. We moved so fast we almost crashed into the front door. I yanked it open and felt a blast of cold night air on my face.

We dashed out of the house into the snow.

A terrifying wind whipped up. The shrieking wind mixed with the ghosts' wailing and screeching inside Hill House.

We ran and ran and ran.

We never looked back.

9

Six months later

It was a beautiful spring day. Birds chirped, and the sun shone brightly on Hill House.

The big Victorian house looked different.

Empty.

The haunted house sign had been taken down. In its place was a FOR SALE sign. Across the printed sign, someone had written in large letters: SOLD.

A young couple strolled up the sidewalk toward the house. A real estate agent walked along with them.

"It's just the kind of fixer-upper we've

been looking for," the woman gushed as they reached the front door.

"We understand they used to give tours here," her husband said. "We heard this place was haunted."

The real estate agent laughed. He opened the door. "Haunted! Right. And I'm a ghost." He laughed again.

The couple giggled and stepped into the house.

The agent followed them inside.

Then he stopped, turned around, and reached for the door handle.

His bald head gleamed in the sunlight.

His tiny black eyes glowed with excitement.

Otto smiled and shut the door behind them.

And the goblin face on the door knocker smiled.

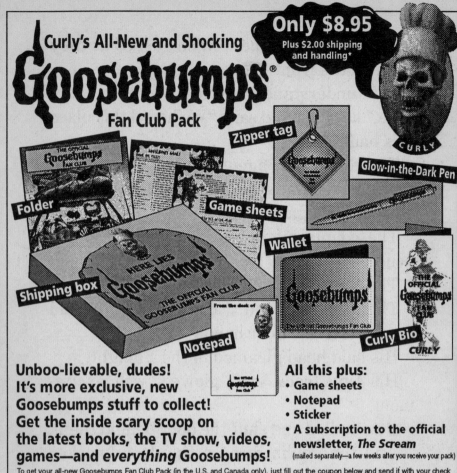